W9-CDV-731

Digger and Daisy
Go on a Picnic

By Judy Young
Illustrated by
Dana Sullivan

Text Copyright © 2014 Judy Young
Illustration Copyright © 2014 Dana Sullivan

Sleeping Bear Press™

315 E. Eisenhower Parkway, Ste. 200
Ann Arbor, MI 48108
www.sleepingbearpress.com

Printed and bound in the United States.

10 9 8 7 6 5 4 3 2 1 (case)
10 9 8 7 6 5 4 3 2 1 (pbk)

Library of Congress Cataloging-in-Publication Data

Young, Judy.
Digger and Daisy go on a picnic / written by Judy Young; illustrated by Dana Sullivan.
pages cm. — (Digger and Daisy; book 2)
Summary: Daisy the dog likes to look at things but her little brother,
Digger, explores every smell as they walk to the park for a picnic, but
after sniffing a hole his nose fills with dirt, leaving him unprepared
for the skunk they meet on the way home.
ISBN 978-1-58536-843-3 (hard cover) — ISBN 978-1-58536-844-0 (paper back)
[1. Smell—Fiction. 2. Dogs—Fiction. 3. Brothers and sisters—Fiction.]
I. Sullivan, Dana, illustrator. II. Title.
PZ7.Y8664Did 2014
[E]—dc23
2013024892

For Milla and Sasha
—Judy

To Dad, who smells ALL the flowers.
—Dana

Digger and Daisy walk to the park for a picnic.

Daisy likes to look at things.

Digger likes to smell things.

And he has a very good nose.

They walk by a garden.

Digger wiggles his nose.

He sniffs. He snuffs.

"What is that smell?" says Digger.

Daisy looks. "Flowers," she says.

Digger puts his head in the flowers.

"They smell good," says Digger.

"Look out!" says Daisy.

"That bee will sting you!"

Digger and Daisy walk by a house.

The window is open.

Digger wiggles his nose.

He sniffs. He snuffs.

"What is that smell?" says Digger.

Daisy looks. "Pie," she says.

Digger puts his nose in the
window.

"It smells good," says Digger.

"Look out!" says Daisy.

Digger jumps back just in time.

Bang! The window shuts fast.

Digger and Daisy walk in the park.

Digger wiggles his nose.

He sniffs. He snuffs.

"What is that smell?" says Digger.

Daisy looks. "Hot dogs," she says.

Digger puts his nose close.

"Look out!" says Daisy.

"It is hot!"

Digger and Daisy walk in the woods.

Daisy stops.

She looks at the ground.

"What is it?" says Digger.

"A hole," says Daisy.

Digger likes to smell everything.

He puts his nose in the hole.

Digger sniffs.

He sniffs dirt up his nose.

Digger snuffs.

He snuffs more dirt up his nose.

"Do you smell anything?" says Daisy.

"No. I do not smell anything now," Digger says.

"My nose is full of dirt."

Digger and Daisy walk some
more.

They see some flowers.

"Can you smell the flowers?"
says Daisy.

Digger sniffs. He snuffs.

But his nose is full of dirt.

"No," Digger says. "I cannot smell the flowers."

It is time to eat.

They sit under a tree.

Daisy gives Digger a hot dog.

"Can you smell the hot dog?"

says Daisy.

Digger sniffs. He snuffs.

"No," Digger says.

"I cannot smell the hot dog."

Daisy gives Digger some pie.

"Can you smell the pie?" says

Daisy.

Digger sniffs. He snuffs.

"No," Digger says.

"I cannot smell the pie."

Soon it is time to go home.

They walk out of the woods.

Digger does not sniff.

They walk out
of the park.
Digger does
not snuff.

They walk by
the house.
Digger does not
wiggle his nose.

They walk by the garden.

Digger does not smell anything.

But Digger sees something.

It is in the flowers.

It is black and white.

Digger puts his head in the flowers.

He sniffs a big sniff.

He snuffs a big snuff.

Then he sneezes a big sneeze.

Now Digger can smell again.

"Look out!" says Daisy.

But Daisy is too late.

Digger smells the skunk.

And Daisy smells Digger!

"You have a good nose, Digger," says Daisy, "but you smell bad!"

Look for
Digger and Daisy Go to the Zoo

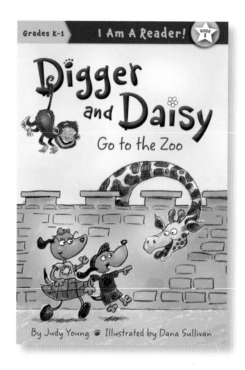

"In this early reader, a dog learns from his sister what he can and cannot do like other animals on a visit to the zoo. . . . It's a lovely little tribute to sibling camaraderie. . . . this work is a welcoming invitation to read and a sweet encouragement to spend time with siblings."

—*Kirkus Reviews*